IF I COULD STAY

BY

STEPHANIE NICOLE NORRIS

To my voracious Queens and Kings, this lunch break series is dedi-cated to you. Thank you so much for reading! I appreciate you more than you'll ever know.

XOXO

- Stephanie

ever did I think I'd be back here. Carmen Mitchell kept her eyes on the home she'd grown up in and left when she was eighteen years old. A myriad of emotions ran rampant through her, and an overwhelming sadness filled her heart at the thought of having to say goodbye to the woman she loved more than herself. Fear seized her nerves at the possibility of facing the boy--now man--she left behind: Dominic Johnson, and although she planned to sneak in and out of town without confrontation, Carmen couldn't deny that a tiny part of her secretly longed for inevitable face off.

"Will thirty be enough?"

In the back of Jesse's Yellow Cab, she studied the white picket fence that surrounded the two-story historical styled home, and a flood of memories assailed her.

"Thirty's fine, ma'am," the bald-headed bearded driver said. "It's twenty-six even if you wanna be precise."

Carmen removed the folded bills she'd taken out of the ATM at the airport and handed them over to the driver.

"Keep the change."

"Thank you very much. I'll get your things."

The driver exited the vehicle and proceeded to remove Carmen's luggage from the trunk, but Carmen couldn't pull her gaze from the green stretch of manicured lawn and the home that sat on four acres of land. In the driveway, several vehicles were unoccupied, and Carmen gathered they were most likely friends of her late grandma Ada Mitchell. It was the only reason Carmen had returned to Brunswick, Georgia, to pay her final respects to the woman who'd raised her.

When Carmen got the call that her grandma had passed in her sleep, it left Carmen with an insurmountable headache, and she'd mourned like a baby in the quiet quarters of her two-bedroom condo back in New York City. As an editorial model, Carmen's schedule was unruly and allowed no room to take trips or vacations. But after getting the news, Carmen dropped everything. The contract she'd signed was in jeopardy of being snatched away from her at that very moment. Carmen would most likely be sued by the company, but with the pain, guilt, and emptiness she harbored, Carmen didn't care one way or the other.

"I never thought I'd be back here," Carmen whispered, bringing her thoughts into reality.

"What's that?" the driver shouted from outside the door.

Carmen snapped out of her haze and slipped the Kate Spade handbag onto her shoulder then exited the cab. Shutting the door behind her, she grabbed the handle of her rollaway luggage and stepped onto the sidewalk, pausing with a lean as her eyes cruised across the lawn once more.

"Thank you," Carmen said over her shoulder. Unhurriedly, she strolled down the walkway, taking the three wooden steps up to the porch that groaned under her weight.

Voices could be heard inside as people talked at a minimum octave. Carmen swiped the thin black strands of hair off her shoulder to rest against her back and straightened her posture before taking her knuckles swiftly against the screen door.

The voices went instantly mute, and the strain of floorboards could be heard as someone neared the entrance. An eye peered out of the blinds that hung against the door's windowpane, and for a second, the person seemed to ponder on whether to receive her or not. Carmen held her breath. Then, there was a switch of the lock and a fumble with the chain as it was removed.

The door swung open, and a pair of aging gray eyes met hers. For what felt like a long mile, the two stared at one another until finally, Carmen smiled softly.

"Hey, Grandpa," she said without making a move to clear the screen door between them.

Carmen's grandfather, Benjamin Mitchell, continued his perusal of his granddaughter. His posture was slightly bent, and the frosted silver strands of hair were sprinkled throughout his head as if he'd been an extra in a rock band in his former life. Benjamin cleared his throat.

"Well if it isn't Ms. America's Next Top Model," his gruff voice groveled.

Carmen's small smile faded, and her lips thinned out. The last thing she wanted was a fight with her grandpa on the day they laid her grandmother to rest. Another round of footsteps could be heard on the floorboard then a second set of eyes were cast over Carmen.

"Carmen, sweetheart?" Donovan Mitchell, Carmen's father, glanced from her to Benjamin, and a frown covered his face. "Come in, why are you still outside on the porch?" Donovan pushed open the screen door and reached for Carmen's arm.

"I wasn't sure if I was welcomed inside."

Donovan's frown deepened. "Why would you think something like that?"

Carmen didn't respond, only cut her eyes back at Benjamin before moving them beyond the foyer to the sea of people who were settled, either in an armchair or on their two feet watching the exchange at the door.

"What time does the funeral start?" Carmen asked.

Donovan sighed. He and his daughter's relationship had been strained for years. Donovan felt partly to blame. He had been only fifteen when her mother Johanna had given birth to Carmen, and the delivery was so risky because of Johanna's young age that she passed away the moment Carmen was introduced to the world. Donovan's parents had taken full custody of Carmen. In turn, Donovan and Carmen grew up almost like brother and sister rather than father and daughter. So it didn't surprise Donovan that Carmen ignored his question, but it didn't hurt any less.

Donovan glanced down at his sterling silver watch. "Um, we should be at the gravesite in an hour." His gaze flipped back over at Carmen, and for an extended spell, they stood eye to eye. Carmen ran a glance over her father's dark brown dreadlocks and those similar features that Carmen saw every day when she looked in the mirror. Heavy light brown eyes were carried under thick brows, a wide nose, and full lips. Carmen tried to release the tension she felt upon walking in the door, but it wasn't easy to shake. She smiled and drew her father in for a hug.

Surprise registered across his face, but the unexpected show of affection didn't stop Donovan's own arms from circling his daughter.

"I missed you, Dad."

The two held each other close, and Donovan breathed a sigh of relief. He still couldn't dismiss the oddness of Carmen's entrance, however. Not now but a little later, Donovan would pull his daughter to the side and ask again.

"I missed you, too, sweetheart."

His calloused hands rubbed up and down Carmen's back then the two parted, and Donovan grabbed the handle of her luggage. "I'll take this to your room."

"No!" Carmen said, speaking louder than she intended to.

Donovan's brows rose. "Why not?"

"I'm staying at the Budget Motel."

"Why would you stay there when there's a perfectly neat and clean room upstairs?"

"Don't pressure the girl," Benjamin Mitchell added. "If she wants to stay at Budget Motel, then that's where she'll stay."

Carmen took her attention back to her grandfather, and the two had another anomalous stare down. Someone cleared their throat, bringing Carmen's attention back in front of her.

"Hey, Carmen, it's been a while. Are you just getting into town?"

Carmen smiled over at Jeremy King. Seeing him made her think of Dominic, her ex-boyfriend. Jeremy and Dominic were as thick as thieves when they were adolescents, but Carmen and Jeremy's friendship had been lukewarm, never really developing into anything meaningful. It made her wonder what he was doing there, and her insides churned at the thought of Dominic being the reason for Jeremy's visit.

Carmen's eyes scanned the room for Dominic, but no one in the room matched the face she'd once recognized as her first love. Inwardly, she breathed a sigh of relief. The last time she saw Dominic was on her eighteenth birthday eight years ago. Her thoughts traveled back to the moment when she and Dominic were just a young couple fresh out of high school.

"Happy birthday."

Dominic produced a fist of yellow lilies that he had handpicked from his mother's garden. A smile flourished across Carmen's face, and her cheeks darkened as heat filled them.

"For me?" she beamed.

"You're the only girl I would risk getting strangled by my mother for pulling her flowers from the yard," he said.

Carmen giggled, and warmth stung her cheeks even more as she gazed into his hazel brown eyes.

"Thank you, Dominic," she crooned.

"You're welcome. I have something else for you, but you can't have it until after your party."

Carmen's eyes widened, and her young thoughts went to the gutter. A hand flew across her lips as she gasped then tinkered out a laugh.

"Not that, nasty girl," he said with a charming grin lacing his lips.

"Okay," Carmen said, "then what?"

Dominic lifted his wrist and glanced at his watch. "In due time, but until then, let's go back inside. I'd hate for someone to think I'm trying to steal you away at your own birthday party."

"Aren't you?"

"Yeah, but I don't want to be so obvious."

They both laughed and stood from the wooden logs they sat perched on. Dominic reached for Carmen's hand, and their fingers linked. As they walked back inside, Carmen dipped her nose to the yellow lilies, feeling giddy at his present but also ashamed of her deceit. She was prepared to move to another city, where she most likely wouldn't see Dominic for a long time, if ever again.

Now just the thought of seeing him once more tightened her gut.

Would it be possible to get in and out of town before that happened? In Carmen's mind, she would pay her respects, grab something to eat, and head straight to Budget Motel before catching a red-eye back to New York. There was nothing in Brunswick, Georgia, for her anymore; well, besides her father, and their relationship was fine with the distance between them. Snapping out of her reverie, Carmen blinked and took an eye over Jeremy's brown hair and pecan eyes.

"Wow look at you all grown up," she said.

He nodded and glanced at Donovan then Benjamin and also noticed the tension. He cleared his throat. "Um, do you have a ride to the gravesite? I'd be willing to take you if you don't."

"Thank you. I could use a ride since I came by taxi."

"Well," Donovan inserted, "You can ride with Jeremy, or you can drive the truck outside."

"Are you talking about that old pickup?" Carmen asked. On her way inside, she'd noticed the black 1972 Chevrolet truck in the open garage. It had been in her grandfather's collection since she was a teen, and from the looks of it, he'd kept it in pristine condition.

Carmen decided not to peer at her grandfather; instead, she smiled over at her father. "Maybe later," she said.

Donovan exhaled and nodded. "In that case, Jeremy you make sure to drive carefully."

"I'm the safest driver in town," he countered.

"Hmm, that's yet to be determined."

Jeremy smirked. "We can get going now if you like."

"Yes, let's go."

Carmen barely glanced at the others in attendance, all too happy to pivot on her heels and head out the door. Jeremy reached for her bag, and they strolled to his Subaru Outback. Carmen slipped inside while Jeremy added her luggage to his trunk. She breathed a sigh of relief and glanced back toward the front door of the historic home. The Outback rocked as Jeremy climbed inside.

"Thank you," Carmen said.

"I've always been able to tell when someone needed rescuing," he said.

"And for that I'm grateful," Carmen responded, removing her eyes from the house over to Jeremy.

He smiled. "It's a part of my job description now." He put the car in drive, and they eased away from the curb.

"What do you do?"

"I work over at the firehouse with Peter Franklin."

He glanced at her. "Dominic used to work there before he became the owner of a chain of hotels. Now he's so busy it's hard to catch up with him."

A ripple crawled down Carmen's skin, and anxiety spurted through her at the mention of Dominic. She wasn't surprised that he was once a firefighter. Dominic had always been the type to help someone, no matter the case.

"Hmm," was all she said.

They rode in silence the rest of the way, and as they journeyed Carmen took in the city, she'd grown up in. The scenery had changed slightly. Where the layout of the town was familiar, some crossroads and intersections had been added. Acres of land, farms, and bred horses that galloped in the fields remained the same, but there were a few businesses that appeared to be new, making Carmen wonder about the town's growing economy.

Jeremy cruised into the entrance of Oak Grove Cemetery, prompting Carmen's thoughts to become consumed with memories of her grandmother. A bittersweet smile tugged at her lips as she pondered on hot summer days when Nana would help her set up the lemonade stand. At the time, Carmen considered it her summer job. It was her first entrepreneurial endeavor with the help of her nana. That was one of the little things Carmen would cherish forever.

Jeremy rounded the vehicle through a circular loop and parked. Just a few feet before them a small gathering of people stood quietly dressed in black and white attire. Carmen inhaled a deep breath.

"Are you ready?" Jeremy asked.

Her nod was slow but assured. "Yes."

Flipping her hair off her shoulders, Carmen reached down into her handbag and removed her sunglasses. She sat them on her face then grabbed the door handle.

"You don't mind if I leave my purse in your car, do you?"

"I can put it in the trunk with your luggage if you'd like."

"I would."

Carmen grabbed her handbag, and they both exited the Outback and met up at the trunk where she locked her purse inside then slowly strolled toward her nana's resting place.

"I don't know how you made it here before me," Carmen said, sidling up to her father's side.

Donovan smiled, but it didn't reach its peak. "Your grandfather's nerves are bad. He drove like that famous race car driver on the way over." At the perplexed look on Carmen's face, Donovan elaborated. "You know, Dale Earnhardt."

Carmen nodded. Her father had always been a fan of NASCAR. It was one of the things she remembered seeing, him settled in front of the television for a day of watching the races.

"Sure," Carmen said, unassured.

Donovan stared at his daughter then slipped his big

burly hand inside Carmen's. Their fingers linked, and they gave each other a sad smile and a hug.

"Grandma's in a better place, you know," Carmen whispered. "I know it's cliché, but if anyone gets in, she does."

The two held their small smiles then Donovan winked at his daughter. When the outdoor proceedings began, only the high-strung voice of the preacher could be heard. After the eulogy, the small crowd was asked to come up row by row to gain their last look at Mrs. Ada Mitchell. It started with the first row where Carmen and Donovan stood holding hands. Benjamin Mitchell moved first, and Donovan followed with Carmen in tow.

Carmen removed her shades just as she made it to her grandmother's casket. Tears slipped from the corner of her eyes, and she had to reach out and clutch her father in a tight hug when Donovan began to break down. Carmen held him close while her father's chest tremored against her own. Carmen's eyes closed then opened and fluttered over to her grandfather standing aside Donovan. Benjamin had a napkin in his hand with tear-filled eyes. He stood solemnly, dabbing the corners with the handkerchief, trying with all his might to hold it together. Benjamin didn't pull his eyes away from his wife, and for a brief moment, Carmen felt sorry for him.

The moment seemed to last forever with no one moving, speaking, or being redirected. The others in attendance held back while the immediate family mourned over the loss of a dear loved one.

The sun shone brightly in the sky, and a small current of wind sailed around them. Irrevocably, Benjamin, Donovan, and Carmen said their final good-byes then trailed back to their seating area. Carmen approached her chair when her eyes traveled over the small sea of people. Her movements slowed then halted as if she were walking in slow motion. Two rows behind her, with his hands tucked neatly inside his pockets was Dominic Johnson. In a white button down long sleeved shirt that stretched over toned shoulders and thick biceps. There was no tie around his neck, and the first button was unclasped as if he gotten hot and snagged it open. The thick pillar of his neck was exposed, and Carmen's eyes lifted to his wickedly sensual mouth, then manly nose to finally rest on the appraisal of his dynamic sturdy gaze.

He stared, unmoving, with dark eyes that pierced right through her. Carmen involuntarily quivered as they held firm, eyeing one another. A riveting wave of warmth slid down Carmen's skin, and suddenly, she was reminded of everything she'd known about Dominic. Memories charged her, and every emotion Carmen thought she put behind her rose to the surface. Her heart didn't pace itself as her gaze washed over him, and unbeknownst to Carmen, Dominic's hadn't either.

There was only a minor instant when Carmen blinked and caught another familiar face in her peripheral, but it was enough for her thoughts to shift and her eyes to cut to a woman standing meager inches away from him. Carmen always prided herself on being an outstanding, intelligent citizen of the community. Even in her younger years, Carmen posed more class than some adults. However, the minute Regan Downing's image crossed her, fear and anger knotted inside Carmen, bringing an instant pain to the forefront.

Before she could stop herself, Carmen was on the move, walking toward Regan in a fast strut.

2

*T*he pace of her stride stirred the crowd slightly as a few eyes watched her cross the short distance to the third row.

"What the hell are you doing here?" Carmen snapped. Her voice was in a hushed whisper, but the longer she stood there, the more her nerves became riled.

Regan's eyes widened, and her thin lips parted as she took a step back.

"Excuse me?" Robert Downing, Regan's husband said. His arm protectively wrapped around Regan, and he pulled her to his side with a frown.

Carmen didn't respond to Robert; her focus was squarely on staring Regan down.

"We should go," Regan said, tugging Roberts' arm.

"Why should we go? We have the same right to be here as she does."

Carmen's eyes cut to Robert, and a hand landed on Carmen's shoulder. She turned to see her father.

"What's going on?" Donovan asked.

Carmen ignored all of their queries, and her focus was turned back to Regan.

"Leave," Carmen said. "Now."

Regan tugged her husband's arm again. "Let's leave. I don't want any trouble."

"No. We're not going anywhere. We've known Ada longer than she has. Hell, no one's seen this girl for a decade, and she thinks she has the nerve to come back and kick people out. No!"

"Stay out of this, Robert," Carmen said, finally showing him some attention.

"I'm in it the moment you put my wife in it. Now listen here," Robert stepped closer to Carmen, getting right in her face, "maybe you should be the one to leave because like I said we're not going anywhere."

The depth of a deep dark voice split through the confrontation like a knife.

"You might want to reconsider your approach, Mr. Downing. Step... back..."

The threat came from Dominic Johnson, and the minute Carmen heard his thunderous vocals, the madness she felt thawed slightly, and her focus was stolen. Dominic moved into the ring and landed a heavy hand on Roberts' shoulder, giving him a nudge backward.

"Don't put your hands on me, boy," Robert said. "This little cunt needs to mind her manners and show some respect to her elders."

Carmen snapped back to Robert and sent a sailing palm across his face in a harsh stinging slap. The group gasped, and Robert pulled back to return her assault when Dominic grabbed a fistful of Robert's shirt and shoved him hard again. The crowd all moved at once just as Robert tripped over his own two feet and fell over the chair into the spread of grass behind him.

"No! Please, we'll leave," Regan said, dropping to Robert's side.

Bewildered, Robert held a finger out to Dominic.

"Someone call the police! I'm pressing charges on you!"

"No!" Regan shouted.

"Excuse me?" Robert said, disconcerted.

"We're not pressing charges. This is Ada's funeral. Let her rest in peace."

Robert went for a rebuttal, but Regan silenced him.

"Please," she said.

Robert's wide eyes flipped from Regan to Dominic and Carmen standing at Dominic's side. "This is not over!" he promised, getting to his feet. Robert stomped through the crowd with Regan scurrying behind him. Everyone watched them trail to their car then get inside and argue as they pulled away from the cemetery.

Instantly, Dominic's attention was turned to Carmen and so was everyone else's.

Carmen glanced around quickly then her eyes settled on Dominic.

"What was that about?" he asked.

Hearing his voice directed at her sent a discordance of chills flying down her skin. Again, Carmen glanced around then without saying a word, she walked away, treading through the crowd and heading back to Jeremy's Outback. Dominic glanced at Donovan, and Donovan shrugged. When Dominic's gaze cruised over at Benjamin Mitchell, the old man only stared back with distaste written across his face. Dominic's thick brows slanted in a frown, and unconsciously, he glowered back at the old man before swiftly turning away to go after Carmen.

AT THE OUTBACK, JEREMY SHUFFLED OVER, AND BOTH he and Dominic acknowledged each other with a head tilt before addressing Carmen.

"Carmen."

It was Dominic who spoke. His voice rode her flesh like silk caressing her skin with a soft touch.

With her back to him, Carmen exhaled then turned around where Dominic arrested her with his gaze. Locked in his connection Carmen's heart, forged a thunderous drum in her chest.

"I'm sorry … Dominic," she paused. "I didn't mean to pull you into anything. You could've stayed out of it, all right." She'd practically snapped at him even as the ever-growing tingling in her belly continued to expand.

Still, with her obvious attitude, Carmen's voice wreaked the same havoc over him as his did to her. Hearing it was like unlocking Pandora's box and releasing everything he'd thought was put away for good over the last eight years. He watched her turn to Jeremy.

"I'm sorry, Jeremy. If you'll open the trunk, I can get my things and head over to Budget Motel."

"How will you get there?" Jeremy asked.

"Why are you staying at Budget Motel?" Dominic interrupted.

Carmen glanced over at him. "Because," she said, "it's where I want to stay."

Jeremy lifted the trunk, and Carmen reached in for her suitcase when Dominic's hand covered hers. He eased in on her swiftly without giving Carmen time to blink before being at her side. A compelling spicy aphrodisiac wafted from him, and her eyes roamed up his athletic chest, to his masculine throat, past his inviting succulent lips, to lock with his dark assessing stare. His nearness brought familiarity that discombobulated her common sense and jolted her nerves. There was concern in the depths of his gaze, and it only shook up Carmen, drowning her in the tornado of emotions she'd wrestled to put to bed years ago. With Dominic came along a shield of warmth; it was like a slow crawling buzz that showered her body and made her heart thump like a piston. Just like that, Carmen dreamed of being crushed by his embrace and taken by the heated encompassing of his mouth.

"If you want to leave, I'll take you to the Marriott, but you're not staying at Budget Motel," Dominic said.

His voice close up had grown more profound, and the warmth that bounced from his lips prickled her skin. Carmen swallowed thickly and struggled to pull her eyes from his hypnotic stare.

"Fine," she said, easing back a step.

Dominic swept an eye over her then clutched her luggage and removed it from the trunk. Right behind him, Carmen gathered her handbag.

"Thank you," she said to Jeremy.

"No problem," Jeremy responded.

Dominic strolled toward his Dodge Durango, and Carmen couldn't help but notice the way his firm shoulders filled the shirt he wore to capacity. She forced herself to snatch her eyes away from the muscular wave of his build, long enough to catch up with his stride to stand at his side.

"You know, I could've gotten a taxi. It's not necessary for you to take me anywhere."

Dominic unlocked his doors and opened the passenger for her.

"Get in," he said.

Carmen hesitated and was caught staring at his mouth.

"Well, are you getting in or not?"

His voice was smooth and even, showing no reaction to her statement. Carmen hesitated a moment more before slipping inside. Dominic shut the door and added her luggage to his trunk then found his way into the driver's seat. He put the car in reverse and drove out of the cemetery, headed toward the Marriott.

"What is your deal with Budget Motel?" she asked. "The Marriott doesn't have any vacancies, trust me, I checked."

"Why didn't you make your reservations earlier then?"

Carmen huffed and sat back in her seat. "Because I didn't know if I was coming or not." She paused. "Until the last minute."

Without offering her a glance, Dominic's thoughts wrestled then shifted in their own battle before he spoke again.

His posture was relaxed, but his jaw not so much. The few times Carmen glanced at him, she wondered what was going through his head. *So much for slipping in and out of town unnoticed.*

"I'm sorry," Carmen said.

The unexpected apology caught Dominic by surprise, but it didn't resolve the anger that had risen to the surface.

"Why are you sorry?" he asked.

Carmen released a sigh. "I'm sorry for leaving the way I did. I never meant to hurt you."

A rushing exhale escaped his lips then he smirked. "Okay, well that settles it then."

"What do you want me to say?"

"Nothing. You don't owe me an explanation."

"You expect me to believe that the frosty way you keep locking your jaw means you didn't want an explanation?"

Dominic smiled, but it wasn't because he found humor in her words.

"It'll take all of twenty minutes to get you over to the Marriott. You're welcomed to ride in silence. There's no need for an apology, or anything else. I didn't want you to stay at the Budget Motel because there's been word of illegal gambling over in that area. The Marriott is in a better part of town."

Carmen stared at his face. "I said I'm sorry."

Dominic pulled to the side of the road and put the car in park. He turned his complete attention to Carmen, and she shifted, forcing her back into the seat in an attempt to escape the wrath she knew he was harboring.

"Why do you want to have this conversation, Carmen?"

"There's no need for us to pretend like we're okay with each other, Dominic."

"Who's pretending? I'm trying to get you to your destination, but *you* are trying something else."

"You needed to hear it. I've had several conversations with myself about how I would explain my sudden departure should we ever meet again."

"Why? To make yourself feel better?" His dark gaze peered into her soul, and a pulsing knot in her throat demanded her attention causing her to swallow. "Well, go ahead. Tell me why you left. I would hate for you to wrestle with sleep at night."

He was being a smart ass, and Carmen knew she deserved it.

"I wouldn't have left if it wasn't necessary," she defended.

Dominic waited for her to go on.

"You don't understand what I went through back then. I needed to leave. I didn't have a peace of mind while I was in Brunswick. It had to be done."

Dominic didn't respond, waiting to see if Carmen would say anything more. She didn't. It appeared as if she wanted to, but her words were lodged in her throat.

"Are you done?" he asked.

Carmen stared into his brown eyes. There was sadness there, hurt, and something more. Regret. Besides that, Dominic's boyish features had transformed into a strong structural face and his mahogany brown skin cut smooth and tight along his masculine formation. Toned arms were noticeably widespread in his thin button-down suit shirt, and it stretched to a cut waist that molded washboard abs against the blanket of material that covered him. He was model material. Carmen could imagine them doing an editorial spread together. Even his hair was perfect for the occasion, with thick black waves that put her in the mind of Trey Songz, dark brows, a piercing golden-brown gaze and full lips that sat succulent for the taking.

"I didn't expect you to understand or accept my apology," she said.

"What did you expect?"

Carmen opened her mouth to speak, but only a rustling breath came out.

"How about we change the subject because there is no end to this conversation that makes what you did acceptable."

Dominic turned back to the steering wheel and put the car in drive. "I've got an idea. Why don't you tell me why you forced the Downings to leave the funeral? What was that all about?"

He re-entered the boulevard and headed off of Mansfield Road. Carmen didn't respond, causing Dominic to smirk and shake his head.

"Or you could ride in silence."

"There are no vacancies at the Marriott."

Dominic exhaled a languorous breath.

"I mean it, Dominic, I am sorry. Look, I was in love with you, okay?"

Dominic pulled to the side of the road again. He released the steering wheel and sat back against his seat with his eyes watching the street in front of him. The tensing of his jaw betrayed his deep frustration, and right in front of her, Dominic's aura began to brood, just as his lids dropped an inch before he took his sharp gaze to her.

"You don't know what love is, Carmen." His voice held an agonized strain. He shook his head once. "How can you talk about love when the definition eludes you?"

Carmen's throat clogged again, and her heartbeat knocked against her breastbone.

"Love is patient, love is kind," he said beginning to quote the bible. "You, are, none of those things."

Momentarily, Carmen's breath was cut off as his words penetrated her psyche. Her chest felt like it would burst, and the chill between them continued to grow.

"So, don't talk to me about love." Dominic tried to rein in his frustration, pulling his gaze away from her and back to the street in front of him. He inhaled and collected himself, and his voice was gruff when he spoke again. "I'm taking you to the Marriott. I own the hotel. You can stay in the penthouse suite. If you decide to catch a taxi from there and go to Budget Motel, then so be it." Dominic reached for the gear shift, and Carmen opened her door then quickly stepped out and twirled around.

"What are you doing?" he asked.

Defiantly, Carmen stared him down. Then without a word, she slammed the door and stepped onto the sidewalk. Dominic put the car in park, and a few curse words slipped from his lips as he removed himself from the vehicle.

"What is your problem?" he said, marching up on her. Carmen stood her ground with her arms crossed.

"I don't want to fight with you, Dominic."

"Well, Carmen, you are not doing a very good job at convincing me."

"I never meant to hurt you," she said.

"Would you stop saying that?" he yelled then just as quickly lowered his voice. "Stop," his eyes faltered, "please."

"No."

Dominic bit down on his jaw.

"Why would you do this now?" he said. "You wait eight years then come back to tell me you never meant to hurt me?"

"I came back to Brunswick because my grandmother died, Dominic! I hadn't planned to see anyone but especially you because I knew you hated me." Carmen's eyes misted over. "But I am sorry. And regardless of what you say, I do love you." A tremor beat through Carmen's chest, and she yielded to the compulsive sobs that shook her. Tears spilled from her eyes as thoughts of her betrayal, mixed with the heaviness of her grandmother's death weighed on her.

The many times Carmen caught herself daydreaming about this moment didn't come close to its actuality. She dropped to a squat and shuffled her fingers through the black strands of her hair, tears falling as she wept.

Standing before her, Dominic's gut tightened, and

her sadness rattled his core. Seeing Carmen threatened his sanity the second their eyes met in that cemetery. It had taken strength to stay focused on the reason he was at the funeral. But when Mr. Downing threatened her by stepping too close, Dominic's attention was thwarted, and a protectiveness he hadn't felt in years resurfaced. The next thing he knew they were in the car together because no matter how bad she'd broken him, Dominic would always do what was right by her. Realizing that made him angry; it was past time that he got over Carmen. She was no good for him. And yet, he mourned with her inwardly for the loss of her grandmother.

Maybe, he'd been too harsh. Maybe, just maybe, he could get over his own pain for a moment to help heal hers. Dominic dropped down to a squat, his thick arms encircling her waist. She leaned into him and allowed herself to be comforted by his embrace. Dominic's knees touched the ground, and he pulled Carmen closer to his chest.

"I'm sorry. You're right. I've made this about us, and you should be focused on your grandmother." He paused as Carmen's tears stained his shirt. "And I don't hate you." He sighed. "I could never hate you."

They detained each other there resting in the ticking seconds of time that passed.

"It would be best if you could get yourself checked in. Then we can talk about it if you want."

It was the best he could do. Dominic was Carmen's

friend first, and that's what she needed right then. Carmen sniffled then pulled her face up to look at him.

"Take me to your place," she said.

Dominic froze, and even his breathing could no longer be heard. Carmen studied him, knowing she'd caught him off guard, but hoping he would oblige.

"I don't want to go to the Marriott or Budget Motel. I want to be with you."

3

"*D*ominic—"

"You can't," he said.

Carmen expected his rejection. "It's the only place I want to go."

"Carmen." Dominic blew out a harsh breath. "You can't just—"

"Do you have a girlfriend?"

"What? That's not why—"

"Does she live with you?"

"Carmen, I don't have a girlfriend."

She almost didn't believe him, unless there was a severe shortage of women in Brunswick, Georgia.

"Then, why?"

"It's just not a good idea."

"You said I need to get settled in. I got right off the

plane and went to my grandparents' house. I could use some tea and a hot bath."

Just the mentioned of Carmen in a bath rocked Dominic's entire axis off balance. He'd noticed her thin waist, and round hips poured into the white blouse and dark suit pants that laced her thighs like latex. Carmen had grown into herself nicely, and Dominic fought with sheer strength to remove the sexual images that tried to assault him.

"I'll be out of here first thing in the morning, and you can pretend this was all a dream."

Somehow the idea of Carmen leaving didn't make Dominic wish it were true, but once more, he tucked his feelings away and stood while pulling her to a stand with him.

"Let's go," he said.

WHEN THE DOOR TO DOMINIC'S LOFT OPENED, HE stepped back, and Carmen entered. Her heel clonked against the industrial-like hardwood flooring, and her eyes scanned the room. There was a rustic warmth in the wooden panels and open layout. It reminded Carmen of some downtown apartments in New York. As her mind mused, a layer of warmth covered Carmen's back when Dominic's elongated frame closed in behind her. He pushed the door, securing it with a lock then spoke.

"If you'll keep straight, I can show you to a room."

His voice held a deep sensuality that cruised over her ear and tickled down her neck. She squirmed and clutched her purse tighter, then her legs moved down the stretch of the corridor. As she walked, her heels clonked over the planks, and at the end of the hallway, Dominic reached around her to open the door to a guest room. There was more of a pinewood smell drifting through its opening. Carmen lifted her nose to the air and took a whiff.

"Mmm, smells good."

"Thank you. There's not a bath in here, but there is a shower. The bath is in my bedroom."

"The shower is fine. Thanks."

"You're welcome. When you're done, come back down the same hallway, and I'll have you some tea ready."

Carmen nodded, and Dominic turned to leave.

"Dominic," she called.

He paused and turned back to her with a questionable lift of his brow.

"Seriously, thank you."

Dominic placed a smile on his face and nodded then turned back and disappeared out of the door.

As soon as it closed, Carmen let out a whistling breath. What the hell was she doing? She paced the length of the queen-sized platform bed with her hands on her hip. It was Dominic. Seeing his agony and feeling it, knowing it was something brought on by her was *too* much for her to bear. Carmen had to fix this, but the way Dominic reacted when she tried the first time was telling. Once he stopped feeling sorry for her because of Grandma Mitchell's passing, he'd likely kick her out on her ass. Carmen had to think fast. She couldn't live the rest of her days knowing he hated her regardless if he said he didn't. His action showed the loathing he felt, and it was uncanny to say the least. No. Carmen couldn't leave this time without fixing things between them, but she had no way of knowing how she could do that.

IN THE KITCHEN, DOMINIC STARTED A BREW OF LIPTON tea and rested a hip against the counter. Twenty-four hours. That's the amount of time Dominic convinced himself he would have to put up with her presence. What disturbed him most was there were two sides of him begging for attention. The side that said he wanted to know everything about what made her leave and was eager to find out if they could pick up where they'd left off. Then there was the other more pronounced side that was adamant about getting her out of there as soon as the sun broke through the sky.

Dominic left the kitchen and strolled through a second hallway that led to his master bedroom. Inside, he entered the closet while unclasping his cuffs and button-down shirt. He removed it swiftly and headed to a dresser where he pulled out a drawer and tugged a white T-shirt over his chiseled chest. Pulling out of his suit pants, Dominic replaced them with Calvin Klein denim. The change of clothes didn't make him any less anxious than the suit had, and Dominic knew why. Carmen Mitchell was in his home. The love of his life, the one he was sure was his future. Could he really spend a night with her and let her leave the next day without that needed conversation?

Dominic braced his hands against the wall and hung his head. For the last eight years, he'd convinced himself that he was much better off. Gone was the broken heart and sleep insomnia he'd endured after her sudden disappearance. Dominic was stronger now. He'd spoken to God, been to church, laid his burden down, and still, his nervous system felt like a runaway train.

"I hope you don't mind ..."

Dominic turned sharply when her voice cruised through his closet. Carmen cleared her throat.

"I, um, decided I'd rather take a bath if it's okay with you."

The sensible side of him was losing the fight. He ran a penetrating eye over her form wrapped in a terrycloth towel. Her bare arms rested at her sides matching his mahogany brown tone unerringly, and her creamy skin shined from her neck, shoulders, to her knees, and toes.

At the entrance of the closet, Carmen prided herself

in not squirming from the virile assessment of his examination. But her heartbeat she couldn't control as it responded loud and clear in disorderly conduct. With her own inspection, Carmen noticed the change in Dominic's attire. His dress down was even more enticing than his suit. The T-shirt he'd slipped over his toned arms was lifted right before it made it to the meeting with his jeans, leaving a peek of mahogany flesh, carved, and on display. A surge of heat drifted over Carmen's skin, and she hadn't given herself a direct order before her feet moved toward him.

The first step was shy and unsure, but the second and third were bold and risky.

"Stop."

It was the only thing he said. Carmen didn't even see his lips move as if the sound had been a thought translated through him. She paused, and her pulse pounded as did his.

Her voice was in a whisper. "Dominic."

"What are you doing?"

His tone was also hushed but profound as he held still.

Carmen's eyes roamed his face then she dropped her head but just as quickly lifted it again.

"Have you ever wondered …" she bit the corner of her lip coyly, "what it would be like to be with each other again?" Carmen took another close step. Two more and she would be near enough to feel the heat radiating from his skin.

"Now why would I think about that?" His gruff voice spoke. Dominic was giving it his best shot to reject her, but still, that sensibleness wavered the closer she became.

Carmen exhaled, it was a minor gut punch, but not one she would let take her out of this fight. She shrugged.

"I've thought about us, more times than I could count. I imagined us waking up together. Seeing your face and smelling your bad breath." She giggled, and the small joke cut through the frost he held.

"I've never had bad breath, girl, so don't play."

Carmen giggled again and took another step.

"There was that time," she tapped her chin, and Dominic's brow lifted sharply. She laughed and shook her head. "I'm only kidding."

"I know you are," he said factually.

Carmen giggled again then took her final step. There she rested in his shadow and was taken by the undertow of his deep stare.

"I've also imagined us making love." Her hands drifted to the tie in her towel, and her fingers worked to remove the knot. On her toes, she lifted, and her soft lips met his, bringing a barrage of warmth spiraling through his core in a tumbling knot. Initially, Dominic didn't return her kiss, but the barrier he detained crumbled with every second that passed. Carmen kissed his lips again then trailed her tongue around his mouth. Like a lightning bolt, a stinging heat shot down his abdomen in a beeline to his groin. With one hand, she wrestled with the knot, and with the other, she slipped her fingers to his zipper and gripped his dick tightly. His restraint was dismantled by her touch.

"Shit," he cursed, capturing her mouth in one breath, and consuming her lips in another.

"Mmmm," she moaned, as a riveting stir of energy coursed through them, taking up root in their chromosomes.

Carmen released his cock and went back to the task of untying her towel just as Dominic's hands dropped to the cloth. Their lips fused, and his tongue invaded her mouth, but still, Dominic held on to the garment, keeping it from revealing her nakedness. Savoring the mouthwatering kiss, he sucked at her soft, wet muscle, and swallowed the sweetness on her palate. Then, with insurmountable vigor, Dominic pulled back, keeping a closed fist on the cloth while his eyes smoldered with stoking fire over her face. His gaze was paranormal, and with all the power in him, he reined in an exasperated breath, then swallowed and lifted his mouth from the closeness of hers.

"This … is not happening."

Surprised, Carmen's brows bunched together.

"Yes, it is. I want you, Dominic, and you want me, too. Why are you holding back? I can tell—"

"Because!"

He hadn't meant to startle her with the loud

outburst, but Carmen was wearing him thin, and Dominic had to regain some sense of control.

"You can't just walk back in here and expect me to what? Where is this supposed to go? You disappeared, and I find out through a Dear John letter that I didn't get until three weeks later that you weren't somewhere rotting in a ditch! Do you know what I went through! Do you know that I died to this world thinking you were gone!"

His voice cut like a wounded animal and Dominic retied the towel's knot.

"This is not happening!"

He sidestepped her and walked toward the exit.

"Dominic!

He paused.

"I'm sorry, okay? I— I ..." She let out a deep breath.

Dominic turned back to her. "You what, Carmen?" He folded his arms.

Carmen walked up to him. "I've missed you since the day I left. I was sick for weeks before I could manage some mobility in my apartment. I need you to understand," she paused.

"I don't know what makes me sadder," Dominic said. "That whatever you went through was so bad that you couldn't confide in me. Someone you say you loved. Or that you came back thinking we could hop in the sack and the eight years of desertion would be forgiven."

Carmen's lips trembled, and she shut her eyes tight and dropped her face into the palms of her hands.

"You're right. You should've known. I realized that too late."

"Why did you leave?"

Carmen swallowed. "You wouldn't understand."

He swallowed his frustration. "Tell me." His voice was even and steady now. "What happened?"

They had a concentrated stare down.

"You wouldn't, understand——"

Dominic ground his teeth together. "How would you know if you never gave me the chance?"

The silence between them lapsed, and Dominic turned to leave when Carmen spoke.

"From the moment I was able to comprehend, I noticed that my grandfather treated me different than other kids. I'm not talking about a little discipline here and there. I mean, it was like he couldn't stand the air I breathed." She paused. "He would give me chores on the farm that would have me working from sunup to sundown. I'd be all alone with no help from anyone. At first, I thought it was something I did that I couldn't remember. I waited for the time when he would surely pull me to the side and chastise me about whatever that was, but that time never came.

"Then one day I overheard him talking to my grand-mother." Carmen's eyes glossed over as the memory drenched her mind.

"No child should be in the field that long. What has gotten into you!?"

"Ada, she's young and has more energy than the both of us put together! You're the only one complaining!"

"That's a damn lie, and you know it! I heard her just a minute ago crying. I saw her rubbing her feet! She looks as if she hasn't had a thing to eat all day. Have you fed her!?"

Benjamin grumbled a response. "No."

Aghast, Ada turned on her heels to march out of the room, incensed with fury. "I'm going to get her right now!"

"No!" Benjamin rushed to his feet. "The girl is fine! She's alive and well, unlike our daughter! So, she should work if she wants to continue living under our roof and eating up our food."

Ada turned back to him, her eyes wide and mouth agape.

"She's twelve years old, Ben!"

"And if she lives past fifteen, she'll be more fortunate than her mother." He leered with an upturned growl of his lip.

"That's what this is about, isn't it?" Ada said. "You blame her for Johanna's death."

When Ben didn't deny it, tears had stung Carmen's eyes.

"It is not her fault," Ada defended, but Benjamin scoffed, turning around to head back to his La-Z-Boy chair.

"Leave the girl where she's at, or I'll put the both of you out."

Snapping out her reverie, Carmen's gaze shifted to Dominic's face as her eyes misted with a fresh wave of tears.

"My grandma did come for me that day, but she didn't have to go far. When she opened the door, there I stood with tearstained eyes, shaking so hard even the embrace of her warm arms didn't calm me. That week we stayed at a hotel. My grandfather was irate but not because he missed us; only because he had to tend to the farm himself.

"My grandmother watched me like a hawk after that. She threatened my grandfather that if he tried something like that again, she would leave him," Carmen snapped her fingers, "just like that. He knew she meant business, and while my nights slaving away at the farm came to a halt, I never missed the way he glowered at me every chance he got. I understood that he hated me and probably wished it was me who'd died instead of my mother."

Carmen shrugged. "I can't say I really blame him. How does a person supposed to act when their child dies during childbirth?"

"Not like a son of a bitch," Dominic growled.

When he'd spoken, the dangerous dip in his voice matched the infuriating mask that was now his face.

"That's not all."

Dominic's brows drew together in an agonized expression.

"I was thirteen ..." she began.

Dominic froze instantly, and his heart almost stopped. Carmen noticed his reaction and put her hands on his shoulders and shook her head.

"No, no, it's nothing like that," she reassured him.

Dominic exhaled sharply and ran a hand down his face.

"You should probably not start with I was thirteen then."

"You're right. I guess I'm just … nervous."

Dominic took another deep breath. "Would you like some tea?"

Carmen smiled softly. "Please."

4

*D*ominic handed Carmen a coffee mug filled with freshly brewed Lipton tea.

"Thank you," she said, blowing across the top of the glass and taking her eye around the open room. There was a piano in the corner stationed against the wooden panel.

Carmen had also noticed gear in Dominic's closet that only firefighters would wear. She cleared her throat and took a sip of her tea.

"Do you still play the piano?"

Dominic's eyes crossed the room to his instrument.

"Yeah."

"Hmmm." She cleared her throat again, knowing she could no longer avoid this conversation. "Remember the day I left school early because I wasn't feeling well. I came down with a fever in class, and Mrs. Robins sent me home because she didn't want me to spread whatever I had?"

"I walked you home," he said, pulling the memory together.

"Yeah, I was tired and out of breath by the time we got here."

"You had the flu," he said.

"And oddly no one in school caught it."

Dominic nodded.

"Well after I went inside the house, I searched for my grandfather. I knew I should tell him I was home, or he would likely blow my head off thinking I was an intruder."

Dominic nodded again, remembering the odd look on Benjamin Mitchell's face at the cemetery.

"Well, I found my grandfather, in the kitchen with Regan Downing bent over the sink."

Dominic's surprise wasn't slight; he stared at Carmen in disbelief.

"Regan's head was practically in the sink, and both of their pants were down to their ankles. I was frozen for too long. Enough time passed that I have a full streaming video in my head of about thirty seconds of my grandfather pounding at Mr. Downing's wife from the back." Her face contorted with renewed disgust. "My grandmother was at the farmer's market. She went the same time every week. When my grandfather spotted me, his first reaction was as if he'd seen a ghost. Then he became angry and shouted at me to get out of there," she said, holding a fist up, pretending to shake it like her grandfather did.

I had to live with him for five years while he screwed Regan Downing every week when my grandmother went to the farmer's market."

"What?" Dominic said, appalled. "So, he continued to do this?"

"Yes, he did. My grandfather didn't care that I had seen them. He probably figured at this point in their lives my grandmother would never leave him anyway. And how could I tell her that her son of a bitch husband was cheating on her every week?" Carmen shook her head. "I couldn't. So I had to put up with it." She took a sip of her tea. "Leaving was the only thing I thought about for a full year. The last one," she added. "I couldn't stay. I needed a fresh start, away from him, away from Brunswick."

"Away from me," Dominic added.

"No, it was never like that."

"Your actions say something else. How could you never tell me what you were going through? I loved you, Carmen. I would've killed your grandfather. Going to jail wouldn't have been so bad, they were only giving fifteen years for murder then. I would've gotten out at what, thirty-five and still had my full life ahead of me."

Carmen gawked, and a hand flew across her chest.

She smirked, but it fell from her face as she studied Dominic's grave demeanor.

"You're serious," she realized.

"You can't think I'd joke about something like this."

Carmen approached him. "Dominic, I was young and feeling out of sorts. The biggest voice in my head was telling me to run. Can you forgive me?" Dominic looked away, and Carmen touched his face with the warm palm of her hand. His gaze was brought back to her. "Please."

Dominic didn't respond.

"At the time, I felt it was necessary to leave. Don't punish me because I didn't have the strength to stay. I'm here now, and I need your forgiveness. Please," Carmen said again.

Dominic bit down on his jaw then released a tumbling breath.

"How can I not forgive you?"

Carmen's heart rejoiced.

"There's nothing I can do about what happened in the past," Dominic said. "I forgive you, but you have to know that leaving the way you did almost killed me." He paused. "In the morning, I'll take you to the airport."

Dominic moved to walk away, but he paused. "I'm sorry for what you experienced. A part of me holds some of the blame for you leaving."

Carmen frowned. "What are you talking about?"

"I was your man, and I had no idea you were hurting." Dominic grimaced. "I missed the mark on that. I'm sorry."

"No, Dominic, I'm not going to let you blame yourself."

"It's okay," he said, "it's the truth."

"We were young. I made mistakes, and you weren't old enough to pick up on things like that."

"Nice try," Dominic said, "but even a child knows when someone they love isn't in good spirits." He sighed. "I'm not looking for a pity party here, Carmen. Just owning my part in our breakup."

Carmen sighed. "I'd like to get to know you, Dominic. I don't want us to be strangers. I can't go back to New York without knowing we're on good terms now or ever."

Dominic stared at Carmen's face as a million thoughts rummaged through his mind. "I don't know if that's a good idea."

"Why wouldn't it be?" Carmen asked. "What do we have to lose?"

"That can't be a serious question, can it?"

Carmen blew out a breath. "Okay, but things are different now. I'm not a child. I understand the dynamics of being in a relationship. So I would never—"

"Chill," Dominic said. "Never say never, and who's talking about a relationship?"

Carmen swallowed a rising lump in her throat, and her thoughts shuffled.

"I just want to be friends," she lied.

The two watched each other closely, trying to find fraud in either of their positions.

"Friends?"

Carmen nodded. "Yes."

Dominic tried to wrap his head around the possibility. Friends with Carmen Mitchell. He was unsure but willing, especially since her arrival had shaken his core. His eyes traveled to the clock on the wall. Time was ticking, but Dominic wasn't sure how much of himself he should divulge. Or if he should walk the fine line of pretense long enough to see her off.

"Okay," he finally said. "Friends." He held out a hand for her to shake. Carmen accepted it, and the bright smile that followed her lips into a sassy curve nearly knocked him over.

"You should go take your bath first and put on some clothes."

"Why, you don't like seeing me traipse around your kitchen in a cotton towel with nothing underneath?"

Her comment sent a flash of heat straight to his groin, and his dick jumped in his pants.

"Chill out on the specifics," he warned, his voice a cloud of thunder.

"Or what?"

Carmen stepped to him and sat the mug she was holding down on the counter. She brushed her body against his and could feel each ridge of his solidly built physique. Dominic had no doubt been in the gym, and his regimen had paid off.

For a brief moment, Dominic wondered if he could hop in the sack with Carmen for a passionate one-night stand of unadulterated bliss, but no. If he wanted to keep his sanity, he knew he couldn't, he shouldn't, and still, Dominic wrestled with the possibility.

5

*H*er closeness was a threat to his libido, and for that reason, Dominic found it necessary to change the subject.

"I'm thinking about going to McArthur's Jazz and Supper Club for amateur night."

Carmen's brows lifted, and she took a meager step back.

"How awesome," she said with a smile.

Dominic was happy she gave him some space; he'd say anything to turn Carmen's attention elsewhere, especially since if they did end up in the sack he was almost sure he would never be able to let it be a mere fling.

"When is amateur night?"

"Tomorrow."

Carmen's eyes perked. "I'd love to come and hear you play."

This idea of Dominic's was beginning to backfire.

"Then, you would miss your flight."

Carmen's bright eyes dampened.

"I don't care, Dominic. I said I want to get to know you."

The softness of her voice wrapped around his heart and tugged. Dominic didn't respond.

"But clearly you care," Carmen added. She held up her hands. "I won't stay longer than I'm wanted. I'm sorry for suggesting it or intruding on your life." Carmen bit her bottom lip then turned quickly and left the room.

A harsh expletive ripped from Dominic's lips. Even with her explanation which was no fault of her own, the years of abandonment wouldn't disappear from his heart. At any time, Carmen could've reached out to him, but she chose to give him silence as if he too were a part of her problem. It still hurt like hell. He needed more time to erase the pain. *Let her go.* His feet held firm as he fought with indecision. On the one hand, knowing her reason for leaving did bring him closure, but trying to open up to her again felt dangerous. However, his fortitude wasn't solid. *Fuck.* He went after her, leaving the kitchen and heading to his bathroom. He entered with her name on his lips but found her naked stepping into a bath. Another concession of profanity slipped from him as his eyes took in the glory that was her creation.

Carmen had always had petite feet and legs, but her thighs were curvier than he'd imagined, and the round fullness of them coupled with the bare apex of her sex became his undoing.

Carmen watched him eat up her form, and his breathing had gone from normal to silent as if he were not allowing air into his lungs. His gaze traveled up to her perky breasts, and his eyes seemed to shade over. Carmen was thoroughly turned on by his perusal, and she leaned her back against the wall and perched a foot up on the edge of the claw-foot tub, further opening her flower.

"Would you like to get in with me?"

She had barely blinked before Dominic was upon her. His arms circled her waist, and his hands dug into her derriere with a herculean grip. Carmen yelped on a gasp, and her legs surrounded his waist. Her hands sank into his neck, and she held on as a wave of wild ripples tore down her flesh, causing her to moan.

"Mmmm."

The hardness of his shaft pressed through his jeans against her mound, and needing to feel his pulsating rhythm, Carmen dropped her fingers to yank at his shirt. They tussled to get it over his head, but it became snagged around one muscular bicep refusing to be tossed. The revelation of his chiseled washboard abs was another heavenly sight to behold, and Carmen pressed her mouth to his skin and licked between the hard pecs in his chest. Dominic shuddered, and Carmen fumbled to get his jeans unbuttoned. When she did, Dominic lifted her and removed them from his cut hips with ease.

Now in his birthday suit, Dominic pressed Carmen's back against the cold tiled wall, and the head of his cock glided across her vagina with a slow dragging dig. Carmen shuddered, and a whimper fell from her lips.

"Is this what you want, Carmen?"

Dominic's voice had grown deeper, and his lips hovered above Carmen's ear with their chests compressed, rising and falling together. His mouth touched her temples, placing a kiss there so tender that it relaxed her bones all the more.

"Is this what you desire, baby?"

Without a chance to change her mind, Carmen was consumed with each inch and blunt fortitude of his extensive dick splitting through her pussy.

"Oh ... my God," she moaned.

Carmen's hands seized his shoulders, and her fingers clenched as they dug into his flesh. Dominic filled her completely, burying himself to the hilt.

"Oh ... my God, oh my God, oh my God," Carmen moaned again. She hadn't expected to be so thoroughly taken. Dominic had surely grown up and not just in height.

He kissed the side of her face while his hips rocked in and out of her womb with a smooth slide. Keeping a firm grip on his shoulders, Carmen screamed as his thrusts tore so deep that she could spark into a billion flames at any second. The heat that covered their skin became a blanket of instant perspiration, and their breathing kicked into gear as did the bump and grind against the solid barrier.

"Oh … Dominic," she purred. "Baby, oh my God," she whined, arching for the fulfillment of his lovemaking.

His grip on her ass spread her cheeks, and he dipped out of her slippery fountain only to lunge back to the base of her canal, again, and again.

"Aaaaaaah! Oh my God, Dominic!

His hips rotated inside her, mixing their flavor as he battered the walls that dared to stop him from shattering their resistance. Carmen's head fell back, parting her mouth giving Dominic the pleasure of consuming her lips with a pervasive hunger that stole her concentration and speared her to another plane. Dominic's strokes enhanced, bullying a drive of powerful thrusts that slapped her senseless in a rock against the wall.

She could've sworn she felt it move as if the solid barrier behind them would demolish with each intensive stroke.

"Dominic!" she shouted. "Ooh my God!"

His mouth latched on to her neck, sucking the warm flesh of her skin to the bone in her shoulders. Carmen screamed and held on for dear life while pleasure was unearthed in Dominic's consumption of her. How they would move forward from this moment remained a mystery, but it was one they would have to endure together.

HER PUSSY HUMMED WITH DELIGHT, AND HER BODY FELT deliciously boneless after they'd reached their climax. Being with Dominic was like riding a supersonic wave that captivated her while simultaneously stealing her breath. The warmth of his hard body against her felt so right, as if she was at home and their loins could finally rest in peace as they joined. The quick trot of their heartbeats matched, and the pulsation at their unification continued to shoot jolts that electrified them both. Dominic dropped his forehead into hers, and his breathing mixed with the labored exhales that she released. His dark gaze pierced her awestruck heavenly face further, warming him on the inside.

"I apologize."

It wasn't the first thing she was hoping to hear after what they'd just shared together, and she opened her mouth to say so, but he beat her to a response instead.

"I wasn't there for you," he continued.

Her eyes shuffled from side to side then found his gaze again.

"How are we back here? I told you it is not your fault."

"And I told you," he said with a deep breath. "Young or not, I was your man. I should've protected you. I love you, Carmen. There's no way in this world your pain should've escaped me. And for that, I'm so sorry."

She went to speak again when Dominic grazed his lips against hers, silencing her rebuttal.

"You were right to leave. No child should endure

what you did. For the longest time, I blamed you. I thought you were," he paused. "Heartless."

Carmen felt his grief, his hurt, his pain, and her eyes closed as his hand trailed alongside her chin. Turning her head to his fingers, Carmen kissed them as they closed in on her mouth.

"I abandoned you without so much as a goodbye." She exhaled deeply. "Let's just say, it was our fault that the relationship didn't work out. I know I've said this before, but the truth of the matter is we were young, and we just didn't know any better."

They were still connected against the shower wall. With his hand, Dominic reached out and turned the knob, causing a steamy shower spray to flow from the head. He covered her in the warm shield of his embrace as his hands dipped to grip her bottom with a stronghold. Pulling them off the wall, Dominic stepped into the clawfoot tub, and the massaging spray immediately threaded a beat into Carmen's backbone.

"Mmmm, that feels so good," she said, lifting just slightly at the caressing drops of water.

"Does it?"

She smiled softly. "Yes."

Dominic held her there while the both them gazed at one another. There was a greater significance to the photographic interchange that they displayed as their eyes roamed the length of each other.

Dominic finding Carmen's womanhood strong, feminine, bold, and alluring unlike eight years before when she was small, with girlish features and hadn't grown into her breasts. Looking at them now, full, perky and heavy with round areolas that begged for his attention was like seeing a butterfly that was once a caterpillar spread her wings and soar.

Suddenly, his attraction to her was more profound and highlighted to the tenth degree. He was proud of her and everything she'd accomplished. After all, it wasn't as if he hadn't been following her career. Regardless of how much he told himself he didn't care, that he was over her, that they had moved on. Still, he picked up a newspaper hoping he would get glimpses of her well-being there. And yes, a part of him hoped beyond hope that she would show up for her grandmother's funeral.

While he wanted the chance to pay his respects to the woman he'd grown to love through the years, he also wanted, no needed, to know why Carmen had left and if he were the reason for her departure. Now being filled with her in a way he dreamed about for years, Dominic didn't know how he'd ever let her leave.

6

*C*armen paused her slow stroll around the grand piano and turned her attention back to Dominic. A freshly brewed cup of warm tea in her hand soothed her palm as she stared at him from across the room. Though their chemistry had always been hot, being with him for the first time in almost a decade changed his image in her eyesight. She didn't see the young boy with aspirations and no fears. The man before her now was of a different breed. Intense, compelling, meticulous in thought. The tortoise instead of the hare. Her thighs still ached from the strength of his touch and her plum still hummed as if it'd been battered for life-sustaining juice. She remembered the immature sex of their youth and fell in awe at the realization that it didn't come close to the earth quaking orgasm that had spilled from her today.

"Remember on my eighteenth birthday when I thought the gift you had for me was ..." She dipped her head and snickered out a heavy giggle.

Leaning his backside into the counter, Dominic crossed his muscular, bare arms as well as his legs, connecting them at the ankles.

"Yeah, you thought I planned to give it to you that night." He chuckled at the memory. "But we never got the chance to that particular evening."

They quieted and engaged in their own thoughts of how crazy it seemed that they would have their first real sexual encounter now instead of then.

"What was it, if you don't mind me asking."

"Ah, see now. That may be something you'll never know."

Carmen gasped. "No fair!"

Dominic chuckled and pushed off the counter to stroll across the room, reveling in the highlight of her eyes. The swag in his trot was strong and tall, carrying the might of a dominant thoroughbred as he settled up in front of her. Carmen's eyes carried over his heavy shoulders, and she admired the cut in his design.

"Maybe I should show you," he paused and peered at her, "maybe not." He rubbed his chin in inquisitive thought.

Carmen's mouth fell. "Wait, you mean you still have this gift?"

Dominic's hand dropped to his pockets where he slipped them inside his pants. He appeared even more masculine standing there bare-chested with his trousers resting at the Adonis belt of his hips.

"Why wouldn't I have it? You don't think I'm the type of guy who would return a gift, do you?"

She opened her mouth to speak, but nothing came out.

Dominic smirked. "Maybe I've always hoped that one day I'd get the chance to give it to you."

He leaned in and kissed her nose, then her lips, hovering there as their warm breaths mingled with electrified tenacity.

"I don't know," she crooned, slipping a lock of hair over her head and out of her face. The strand would not be disturbed as it fell back across her eye. Dominic chuckled and ran the loose tendril behind her ear. His warm fingers trod along her jaw as he cupped her face and pulled just enough to give a silent order. She obeyed, lifting her lips to meet his heavy full chops head-on. They watched each other as their lips sealed, electrifying their connection. She exhaled into his mouth, feeling as if she were floating on a cloud. The rapturous way he sucked her in, stole her soul, keeping her fulfilled simultaneously. It was heaven sent. Without touching her, Dominic's authority pulled her in with a magnetism that sealed her chest against his. The cup of tea in her hand was forgotten. She had no idea where it went. Carmen hadn't noticed when Dominic removed it from her hand and placed it on the piano. It escaped her because the warmth from the cup had been replaced with the heat from his entire aura.

She trembled when a hot wave covered her body, making her aware of his strength and saturating her with the warmth of his embrace. His nearness kindled feelings of fire that trailed along her feet and strolled up her thighs where her pussy creamed for him.

"When we were in the bathroom, you said you loved me," Carmen spoke against his mouth. Her voice was heavy, throaty even, and she cleared it in an attempt to recognize herself. Dominic licked his lips and drove his gaze in a trace over her pillowy mouth.

"Yeah, so …"

"You didn't use past tense like you did in our earlier conversation."

Her heart beat erratically, and her nerves tensed as anxiety spurted through her.

"What are you asking, Carmen?"

Her mouth sealed, and she backpedaled on her thoughts. A smile, tentative and coy spread across her face. Without saying a word, she shook her head, deciding it was best that she didn't know in the case his answer wasn't what she sought.

They stood there, body to body, but their hands rested at their sides. There was an inner struggle. While they agreed the demise of their relationship was shared, still, the inevitability of them separating again was as true as the day was long. Here they were, reunited and feeling renewed about their friendship.

They already indulged and found refuge, forgiveness, and release in one another. Even with the harsh reality of their breakup, there was no love lost. In fact, that was the thing that stood before them now. Love. It was as deep as the depths of their gaze and as potent as the fire that burned within them. But still, neither of them spoke about it for fear that it would only tear them to shreds when the time came for them to part, again.

Dominic knew what Carmen wanted, and he was inclined to give it to her. Yes, he still loved her, now and forevermore. But was it really what she needed to hear? What good would it do if they couldn't be together?

"Stay here," he said.

Carmen's eyes lurched, and her pulse quickened. "Wha—?"

She watched him walk away, through the open living room to disappear around the corner. When he was no longer in her sight, she inhaled a shaky breath. His 'stay here' was telling her to stay put in her position, and yet, Carmen couldn't help but feel an overwhelming sadness that it hadn't held a different meaning.

What the hell was she going to do now? Getting on a plane and coming to Brunswick had been a strain in the beginning. But now catching a red-eye back to New York seemed to pale in comparison. Carmen had always known that she was still in love with him, but being here now, experiencing the way her heart hammered in his presence and the magnitude of sorrow she felt knowing she would have to leave was such a burden that she could fall where she stood.

She sensed his movements before he reappeared. Dominic hit the corner with a swagalicious stride that accelerated her pulse and drummed her heart. His return was like opening a new gift on Christmas morning. She almost missed the box in his hand that was covered in a golden wrap with a red bow attached.

A smile scurried across her lips, and again Dominic reveled in the highlight of her face.

"For me?"

He crossed his eyes and stuck his tongue out, making her laugh.

"Nah, for the girl behind you," he teased.

"Shut up!"

Dominic chuckled and handed her the gift.

"Happy Birthday," he said.

They stared at each other with the moment being a surreal revelation. Eight years ago, he'd never gotten the chance to give Carmen her birthday gift. She'd disappeared into the night like an apparition never to be seen again. Her hands wove over the cool wrap, and she fingered the lace of the bow.

There was a sudden knock on the door. They both turned to the sound.

"Are you expecting company?" Carmen asked.

"No."

He strolled across the room, cutting around the sofa to approach the door. He opened it without checking the peephole, and on the other side, Sandra Johnson, Dominic's mother smiled with delight.

"Hey, baby, I brought you dinner."

She stepped inside with the handle of a lunchbox cuffed in her fingers. When her eyes flipped across the room, she paused.

"Oh, I didn't know you had company." Mrs. Johnson smiled. "Carmen, is that you?" Her gasp was a soft slow inhale followed by a wider smile that brightened her eyes with a twinkle.

"Yes, ma'am, how are you?"

"Wow," Mrs. Johnson said.

Dominic closed the door and took the lunchbox off his mother's hand. Sandra Johnson had had a habit of bringing him lunch as a reason to check up on him and make sure he was okay. It was no secret in his family that the disappearance of Carmen had shattered him so thoroughly that there were days he'd lock himself in his apartment to hide out.

Mrs. Johnson turned to her son. "Well, I won't stay. I just stopped by to bring you nourishment. However, I stopped by the auto mart and grabbed a few cans of oil because my light came on. Can you check it out for me?"

"Of course."

Dominic sat the food down and went out to check the oil. Mrs. Johnson strolled slowly across the room, her eyes dashing over Carmen in easy detail. Mrs. Johnson looked as youthful now as she had years ago, and her petite frame hadn't gained a pound. The gray and white spaghetti junction of thin curls wrapped around each other and rested on top of her shoulders, and the only thing that had been added to her appearance was the bifocals that perched on top of her nose.

"I knew you'd be back one day," she said. "Even though you think this is about Grandma Ada's funeral, it's not. God always has plans different than our own, and sometimes it takes a while for us to recognize that."

Carmen didn't want to disappoint Mrs. Johnson, but it was best that she be upfront with her. "I'm sorry for the way I disappeared."

Mrs. Johnson shushed her. "We all have to go our own way before we make it to where we're meant to be."

"But, I'll only be here for today. I'm leaving tomorrow."

Mrs. Johnson smiled. "Sure," she said, holding that same twinkle in her eye.

Dominic reappeared, and the door shook as it closed behind him. "You're good, Mom. When I checked, the light wasn't on, and the oil appears to be almost full. I poured a bottle in any way."

"Thank you, baby."

She glanced at Carmen. "See you later," she said.

As Mrs. Johnson passed Dominic, she reached for his face and caressed it softly. "I'll see you later, too."

Dominic kissed her on her temple and walked Mrs. Johnson to the door where she exited with a small lingering smile on her face. The door clicked when he closed it, and Dominic returned to Carmen with an upturned brow.

"Did I miss anything?" he asked.

Carmen smirked and shook her head. "No." She'd decided to keep Mrs. Johnson's comments to herself. Besides, if his mother wanted him to know, she wouldn't have sent him on that wild goose chase for oil.

"Open it," Dominic urged, in reference to Carmen's unopened gift.

An unencumbered smile rose at the corner of her lips, and she turned her back to him and sat the box on top of the grand piano. With a single pull of the lace bow, it became undone, and suddenly the excitement of what lied beneath made her rip the paper to pieces. Dominic's mouth widened as Carmen laughed, finding joy in opening the present. A royal blue box with a chrome microphone pictured on the front with the words Samsung underneath were revealed. A gasp so sharp flew from Carmen that it nearly took her breath away. Slowly, she turned around to him as a mist of tears clouded her vision.

"We were at the eighth-grade dance, our peers had voted for king and queen, and those two people had to either dance together or create a duet," Dominic said. "You were shy, and afraid that people would think you were a fast tail girl if they witnessed us dancing together." He stepped closer to her. "So, with your talent of song and mine with the piano, we put on a show for the crowd. You sang—"

"'Fallen,' by Alicia Keys," Carmen said, lost in the memory.

Dominic nodded. "And I stroked the keys to the tune as your voice serenaded the audience."

"It was so beautiful. The crowd was swept away. I'll never forget their faces."

"Or the standing ovation you received afterwards," he said.

"We," she said. "We received a standing ovation."

Dominic nodded. "You have the voice of an angel. Why didn't you go after your dream of being a songstress?"

Carmen sighed. "It's not easy to get into the music business. I mean modeling isn't either, but after doing the modeling competition TV show, more opportunities for modeling came about." She shrugged. "And I just went with it."

Dominic nodded. "That's understandable."

"What about you? I was so surprised when Jeremy told me you owned a chain of hotels. Are you just getting into your dream of being a musician?"

Dominic folded his arms. "When did Jeremy tell you I owned a chain of hotels?" he said with a significant lift of his brows.

"Oh, um … when he gave me a ride to my grandma's funeral." She sighed as memories of Ada Mitchell mounted once again in her mind.

"What else did he tell you?"

Carmen shrugged. "Nothing really."

"Nothing really, or nothing?"

She cleared her throat. "He told me you used to work at the firehouse with them, which didn't surprise me."

"Why not?"

"Because you're that type of guy. The kind that loves to help."

They watched each other for a quiet moment.

"I want you to see something."

He reached for her hand and pulled her toward the door.

"Are we leaving?"

"Yeah."

"Wait, let me grab my bag and microphone in case this is your way of kicking me out." Her laugh was short-lived as Dominic wrapped her in his arms with a quick whirl. "Eek!" she screeched, caught off guard by his sudden movement.

"If I wanted to kick you out," he said, his lips seconds away from hers, "then I would just do it, but we've established our faults and moved past that, right?"

She nodded, and he peered at her until she used her words.

"Yes," she said, knowing what he wanted.

"Carmen, I know we haven't been around each other, but you should know I'm a man of my word, and I'd like to think that my actions match them. So, you don't have to wonder if I'm going to do or say something quick-witted or backhanded. Did you trust me back in the day?"

"Of course."

"Do you trust me now?"

"Yes."

He stared at her then leaned forward, dropping a slow lingering kiss on her cheek. A quiver waved down her flesh, and she closed her eyes and inhaled his scent.

"Let's go."

7

*T*hey say time flies when you're having fun. That truth became a reality as Carmen glanced down at her smart device. Her phone read six-thirty in the evening, and her flight was set for five a.m. She gnawed on the bottom of her lip, thinking of what awaited her back in New York. Her modeling career, new friendships that had now become close to her heart, her condo in downtown Manhattan. But it wasn't the only thing that awaited her. The glitz and glam would be met with an emptiness that she didn't want to recognize. Thinking about what she'd be leaving behind made her chest suddenly feel heavy.

It was at that minute that she glanced over at Dominic. The side profile of his mounting neckline and the noticeable veins in his arms and hands underlining his strength amped her nerves. She thought of the way his fingers dug into her skin, and the unrestricted pounding of his pelvis to her pussy when they made love. A shiver slipped over her body, and she bit down on her jaw as the reminiscence of his tongue exploring the inner recesses of her mouth spawned like that of a cinema. He navigated the city streets, going in a direction that pulled her from the passions of her musings and torpedoed her back to a time that highlighted their youth.

"What are you thinking?" Dominic asked.

"What makes you think I'm thinking anything?"

"Because it's written in that faraway look in your eyes."

She chuckled. "You're driving, how do you know about—"

Her sentence was disturbed when Dominic's dark gaze touched her entire body from across the seat. Like a spicy yet full-on caress, his eyes drove over her, making no mistake to answer her question with a mere look.

Carmen swallowed, and her pussy thumped.

"Just because we've been a part for a while doesn't mean our connection was severed. I knew you'd be at the funeral the same way I've felt you staring off in thought, down at your phone, and over at me while I've been driving. Now," he said, "are you going to answer my question?"

Carmen puckered her lips. "So, you think you know me, huh?"

"Do you think I know you?"

A short silence lapsed between them.

"I've watched you from afar. I saw you on the modeling show. You were great, as I always knew you would be. The newspapers around here featured your accomplishments on a regular basis. The town of Brunswick was happy to have you as one of their natives."

"Is that so?"

"It is. As a matter of fact, when you won the competition, the town celebrated your achievement. There were parties thrown at just about every bar with the biggest one over on Jekyll Island."

Carmen smiled softly, feeling honored that her town had celebrated her win. It was one of the biggest moments of her life. She'd never forget the feeling. It had solidified her in the modeling world and catapulted her into a life of high fashion where she'd run the catwalk with notable models as great at Tyra Banks and Naomi Campbell.

"And what about you?"

Dominic glanced over at her then pulled in front of The Keepers Dwelling on St. Simon Island where he put the Durango in park.

"What about me?"

"Did you also celebrate my victories?"

Dominic sat against the seat and held her stare.

"You already know the answer to that question, yet you ask it anyway. Why?"

Carmen ran the rim of her teeth across her bottom lip.

"We are more alike than we are different," she said.

He arched an inquisitive brow.

"You know the answer also, and still you asked."

A slow rising smirk quirked at the corner of his lips.

"I asked because I want to hear you say it. Did you celebrate my victories, Dominic, or were you too busy hating me?"

Dominic reached for his bearded chin and rubbed it in thought as if he needed a moment to process her query. He didn't but letting her know how he felt during that phase in his life would open him up to a new set of vulnerabilities, and Dominic didn't think that would be wise considering he'd most likely never see Carmen after today.

The beat in his heart knocked with an overactive flutter at the thought of losing her again, but what could he do about it? Asking her to stay seemed premature. Carmen had built a life in New York. Everything she knew now was there, except for him. Dominic resigned that he'd have to get over it. Some things were never meant to be.

"Well?" Carmen asked, still waiting for his response.

"Come," he said, opening his door and ignoring her question. "I want to show you something."

He removed his long limbs from the truck and strode to the passenger side where he opened the door and helped her out of the vehicle. Their fingers intertwined, and Dominic pulled her close, shielding her in the warmth of his broad chest.

"I haven't been here in forever," Carmen said as her heart teetered behind her breast from his proximity.

"I thought you might like to see it before you leave. It was once one of your favorite places."

Carmen smiled warmly, and Dominic shut the door behind her. He removed himself from her front, and hand in hand, they strolled up the brick path to The Keepers Dwelling where they climbed the porch and entered the door.

Hardwood floors, traditional style furniture, and thick columns were just a few of the features inside the Victorian structure. The Keepers Dwelling currently served as a museum that incorporated interactive exhibitions, extraordinary artifacts, and rooms that were a timestamp in the history of St. Simons Island along with the residence of the periodic lighthouse keeper.

The remembrance of the place struck a chord in Carmen, and her fingers naturally flexed to tighten around his. Dominic glanced over at her.

"You all right?"

"Yeah, it's just bringing back so many things."

"Yeah? Check this out."

They exited through an extensive corridor and climbed the one hundred and twenty-nine steps to the top of the lighthouse. Another awestruck gasp left Carmen as her mouth fell open at the view. With one hand tucked inside Dominic's, she took the other across the steel railing.

"This is just as I remember it but even more

breathtaking."

The panoramic view of the coast made Carmen feel like a bubbling teenager again. Her heart hammered as she took in the sight, and the warmth that cuddled her didn't come from the warm brisk of air but from the man who shared her space.

"Thank you for this. After seeing my grandmother for the final time, I really needed this." She glanced up at him. "I mean it, Dominic, thank you so much."

Her words were heartfelt, so much so, that Dominic's heart just about marched out of his chest. Her brown eyes held a subtle glow in the soft sunset, and her beautiful features were accentuated as she gazed up at him.

"You're welcome. I also wanted you to see this."

He spun her around and pointed to the corner of the structure where she gasped again, and her hand flew to cover her neck. With wide eyes, Carmen glanced back at him.

"That can't be what I think it is!"

Now, his heart beat triple time at the exuberant lightening of her entire face.

"It is," he said, "our initials are still carved there where we put them eons ago. Even throughout the years, where most of this place has been renovated, this remains."

"Oh my God."

Carmen removed her hand from his and rummaged through her purse in search of her cell phone. She fished it out and opened the camera then dropped to a squat and took a picture of the engravings. She laughed while she took snapshot after snapshot, amazed that the signature stamp was still there.

Finally, she rose to her feet and was met by Dominic's studious stare. His gaze weighed gently on her, as if taking its photographic shots in an effort to save her sweet memory in the case that this would be the last time they were together. Carmen dropped her phone in her purse and framed his face with her hands.

"I could just kiss you!"

Without thinking about it, she pushed to the tips of her toes and sank her lips against his warm mouth. Where a part of him needed to stop her; after all, they'd done so much already, anything more would just begin to blur the lines of their situationship, he couldn't. The softness of her breasts and stomach felt so right pushed against his torso and with it a spiraling heat ballooned against his crotch. His arms covered her waist, and with a small amount of cock-strong strength, he planted his fingers in her spine and pulled her closer. His dick sprung to life as his tongue invaded her mouth with a velvet swipe against her own.

"Mmmmm," Carmen moaned, now fully aroused. The peaks of her nipples hardened, and the stronger Dominic's hold became, the tauter her areolas did.

With sheer strength, Dominic pulled from her mouth and removed his body from hers. It was quick, as if he'd been burned and the index of heat caused him to flinch from the flame.

"We should probably," he cleared his throat, "chill."

To say Carmen was a little confused was an understatement, but she didn't look for an explanation. She nodded once but didn't say another word.

"Are you hungry?" he asked.

She swallowed and found her voice. "I could use some food."

"I know a place."

"You think?"

Dominic chuckled. "Yeah …" he drawled, "let's go."

He reached for her hand, but Carmen was hesitant to take it. If he were having second thoughts about their reunion, she didn't want to be the last to know.

But instead of ruining the moment with more questions, she only nodded and strolled next to him as he led the way back to his truck.

INSIDE THE DURANGO, THERE WAS AN AWKWARD SILENCE that Carmen was dying to break, so she just went for the first thing that came to mind.

"Where are we going?"

"I don't know, what are you hungry for?"

You, she thought.

But she said, "I don't know, nothing fancy, maybe a good ol' greasy cheeseburger."

Dominic smirked. "Are you allowed to eat those? I know models have to stay in tiptop shape."

Carmen nodded. "True that, that's why I want one because I haven't had one in forever. And," she said, lifting a finger, "even if I wanted to sneak and eat one, I couldn't because Devon would never have it." She chuckled.

"Devon?"

"One of my nagging friends," she said. "He swears he knows me more than I know myself."

"Is that right?"

"Yeah. I try and pay him no mind half the time, but he has a key to my condo."

Dominic raised a thick brow.

"For emergencies," she added for clarification.

"Hmmm," he mused, turning another corner before pulling into the parking lot of Brogen's, one of St. Simon's burger bistros. The bar and grill was an open-air diner with views of the ocean built on two levels of wooden beams.

Carmen jumped out of the truck and took a whiff of the air before Dominic had a chance to make it around to her.

"I can smell the food from here," she said. "Delightful."

"Wait until you try their burgers." Her stomach growled, and Dominic chuckled. "Come on before you starve. When's the last time you ate anyway?"

Carmen searched her thoughts. "I had a straw-berry crème cheese bagel for breakfast if that counts."

Dominic frowned. "Hardly," he said, placing his hand at the small of her back.

The sensation from his palm elicited a riveting round of heat that drove down her spine and made her squirm on her feet. She looked up at him as he glanced down at her.

"Shall we?" he asked.

She nodded, and they entered the establishment.

8

*D*ominic and Carmen had barely gotten comfortable at a table when a server approached.

"Welcome to Brogen's, I'm Grace Miller, and I'll be your waitress today. How are you two doing?"

Dominic glanced at Carmen. "Much better now," she said.

"Oh?"

"Yeah, I'm in town for my grandma's funeral, but a good friend of mine has been keeping my mind occupied." Carmen glanced from the server to Dominic.

"Sounds like a great friend."

Carmen nodded. "I agree."

"I'm sorry about your grandmother. Let me know what I can get you, and your meal's on the house."

"Oh, you don't have to do that."

"Of course I do. Besides, my husband owns the place." Grace winked, and Carmen smiled softly. "Both of your meals are complimentary. I'll give you a minute to look over the menu, and I'll be back."

"Thank you," they said in unison.

Grace left the table, but neither Dominic nor Carmen shifted to study their menus.

"Do you know what you want already?" Carmen asked.

"Yeah," Dominic said, but his need didn't derive from food associated with the menu. "Do you?"

"I told you before I want a cheeseburger."

Dominic chuckled. "That's right, maybe you should take a look and see if they have specialty cheeseburgers. Their food comes in a hefty serving, so you may want to check to be sure."

Carmen took his word for it and studied the menu.

"Hmmm, you were right," she said, looking at the significant helping of food. While she considered the options, Dominic reviewed her but simultaneously tried to ignore the constant tug in his chest.

"Devon sounds like someone who's near to your heart," Dominic blurted.

Carmen lifted her eyes to look at him, and in a slow rock against the back of her chair, she relaxed against it.

"He's a good friend. Someone I trust."

Dominic nodded but didn't respond. In actuality, he didn't know how to. Where he wanted to question her to death, it wasn't really his place. Still, he couldn't help but know.

"How long have you known him?"

Carmen shrugged. "About four years I guess, give or take."

Dominic nodded again, and this time, he glanced around the establishment as if needing to take a break from watching her sultry gaze linger on him with question.

Grace returned to the table.

"Are you two ready to order?"

"Yeah, can I mix your sautéed burger with your cheddar bacon burger?" Carmen asked.

"Sure thing, so you want the sautéed onions, mushrooms, and melted swiss on top of bacon and cheddar cheese?"

"Yeah, except I don't need a double dose of cheese, so the swiss will do."

"Nice choice."

"And for you, sir?"

"I'll have the same," Dominic responded.

"Drinks?"

"Water for me," Carmen said.

"Water for us both," Dominic reiterated.

"Okay, I'll return shortly with your drinks."

"Thank you," they crooned.

"Not a problem." Grace took a closer look at Carmen. "You wouldn't happen to be that model who won the—"

"Yes, that's me."

Grace gasped. "I knew it! I told Sterling it was you sitting out here." Grace's smile stretched the length of her face. "Well congratulations. Just so you know, we were excited to find out one of our own had gone on to make it in the big city. How's modeling working out for you?"

"It's been a whirlwind for sure, but I love it, wouldn't change it for the world."

"Oh, I'm sure. Staying in New York must be pretty sweet, too. I hear it's expensive, but when you've got an unlimited bank account, it must be quite a ride, huh?" Grace wiggled her brows.

"I don't know about having an unlimited bank account, but—"

"Oh!" Grace waved Carmen off. "Surely, you're just being coy. But I won't get all in your business. Are you in town for good?"

"Until morning."

Carmen glanced at Dominic then looked back to Grace.

"I've got a red-eye at five."

Grace whistled and glanced at Dominic. "Don't keep this one out all night, or she'll miss her flight."

Dominic's smile was the most unauthentic beam Carmen had ever seen.

"I won't," he said.

Grace nodded happily. "Okay, sorry about the mumbling. I'll be back with your food."

Grace scurried away from the table, leaving Dominic and Carmen to muse over her upcoming flight.

"So five a.m., huh?"

Carmen nodded. "Yeah," she said uneasily.

"Well it was nice getting to know you again."

His words were final and came out a bit sarcastic.

"Dominic, I don't want this to be the end of our friendship. I can give you my number. You can call or visit whenever you like."

She bit her bottom lip, and her chest tightened just thinking about the departure. In response, she cleared her throat.

"It's probably best if we leave things the way they are," Dominic countered.

There was a noticeable pain in her chest. "So you don't want to be friends then?"

"Do you think Devon will agree with you being friends with your ex?"

Thrown off, Carmen's eyes bucked, and her mouth dropped. "Devon? Why would I care what he thinks?"

"You said you trust him, right. He has a key to your place. He's someone important to you. A boyfriend, or maybe just a close friend. Either way, I can't imagine he would be happy about you talking to me, and especially not visiting."

"If that were the case, then that would mean I've cheated on him with you. What kind of woman do you think I am?"

Dominic didn't respond, which frustrated Carmen.

"Look, Devon isn't my," she paused, and Dominic eyed her, waiting for her to finish.

"You know what, you never answered my question about if you celebrated my victories while I was away."

Dominic blew out a whistling breath and turned his gaze away from her again.

"Are we seriously back here?"

"Yes, we are because you're asking a lot of questions but answering none of mine."

Grace re-approached their table, and, in her hands, she balanced trays, one carrying their drinks and the other carrying their food.

Rising to his feet, Dominic took a tray off her hands as Grace sat the spread of food on the table before them.

"Thank you," Grace said to Dominic. Grace glanced over at Carmen. "Well, he's a helpful fella, isn't he?" Grace winked. "If you need anything else, just give me a holler." She strolled away from the table with the two empty trays in hand, and Dominic reclaimed his seat.

"Well?" Carmen spoke, wanting to get back to their conversation.

"What difference does it make?" Dominic said.

Carmen folded her arms. "You're still mad at me," she said. "What was all that you said at the house about us acknowledging that the demise of our relationship was both of our faults? What was the purpose of saying that if you were just going to act like this?"

"What am I acting like, exactly? The only thing I've done was say I don't think we should seek a friendship past tomorrow morning after I drop you off at the airport. How am I being some type of way by saying that?"

"Are you serious?"

In response, Dominic only stared at her with a probing concentration.

"After everything we shared today, you could let me leave and never speak to me again?" Her voice nearly cracked when she'd spoken, and Dominic could feel her pain from across the table. In turn, his own heart was causing a ruckus in his chest that nearly drove him to the point of insanity.

"You should eat your food before it gets cold," he said, ending the conversation before it could go any further.

They had an intense stare down then quickly Carmen pushed from the chair and stood to her feet.

"I've lost my appetite," she said, walking away from the table.

"Where are you going?"

"To the ladies' room."

She disappeared quickly, and Dominic cursed profusely. What did she want from him? A long-distance relationship? No. It wasn't something he could do, not with her anyway. The madness that boiled within him wasn't because of her disappearance. Since that had been explained, he'd only felt responsible and guilty for never being there for her regardless of the fact that they were young and ill-equip to understand the dynamics of a relationship. In his heart, Dominic wanted to make up for it. Somehow, he wanted to spend a lifetime showing and proving that he could be her protector, her council, her provider. He felt a raw need to prove that she was meant to be with him, and him alone. Not Devon or anyone else who'd caught her eye.

However, in his mind, Dominic couldn't bring himself to the point of asking her to stay. She would have to give up everything she worked hard for. Her new friends, career, her entire life was a world away from here. It would be the selfish thing to do, and God if he didn't wrestle with it.

Dominic spotted Grace strutting past the table; she glanced over and paused.

"Everything all right, how's your food?"

"If you don't mind, can we get to-go boxes for the food?"

"Sure thing."

Grace went back the way she came. When Carmen returned to the table, Dominic had packed the food and was on his feet, prepared to go in search of her.

"Are you okay?"

His voice was caring with a note of concern.

Carmen nodded. "I'm tired, I think I should lie down for the evening. You don't mind, do you?"

His gaze traveled over her face, noticing her puffy eyes. "Have you been crying?"

"No," she said quickly. Too quickly.

"Are you lying?"

Carmen pulled her gaze away and took them on a voyage around the room.

"Can we just go, please?"

Dominic hovered there, watching her a moment longer before nodding once and leading her out the door.

9

The car ride to Dominic's was as silent as the midnight hour with the both of them shuffling through thoughts that almost mirrored the others. Fifteen minutes later, they pulled into his driveway, and Dominic cut the engine. Another second scaled by, and they both sat, continuing to mull over their musings. She had questions but couldn't find her tongue to ask them. He wanted to speak but didn't know what difference his words would make if spoken. The wrestling in their spirits practically consumed them in the darkened silence of the car, but alas, after much consideration, they both exited without a single word.

Stepping into his place brought back memories of their earlier tryst. The abandoned cup of tea sat still on top of his grand piano. It reminded Carmen that she'd wanted to stay and watch him play at amateur night the next day, but Dominic had made it clear in no uncertain terms that she shouldn't miss her flight. It was then that the fight in her reached a boiling point, and unable to hold steady, Carmen could no longer stay silent. She turned to him and folded her arms then stepped into his face.

"So that's how it's going to be?"

"What?"

"You heard me. Just like that, you're going to make love to me, tell me that you forgive me, admit your fault in our breakup, take me out to that lighthouse, then tell me you never want to see me again!?"

She was furious. The audacity of him to throw her emotions into a tumult of activity then slam the door in her face was so cruel.

"How could you do this, Dominic? Why would you? It's clear we both still have feelings for each other, but you're like a stubborn bull that refuses to open up! Why won't you answer the questions that matter to me, huh? Did you celebrate my victories? Were you happy for me? Why didn't you pursue your musical career, huh!? Tell me. Stop holding back and tell me now!"

"Yes, okay! I did celebrate your victories, with tears falling down my face in the privacy of my own home because I felt like you had to get away from me in order for your dreams to come true!"

His confession snatched her breath and rocked her entire soul.

"I couldn't do anything after you left. I lost my desire

to follow my dreams because my dream was being with you. Not playing the piano. Not owning a chain of hotels. Not being an all-star NBA basketball player. It was you, okay!? It was always you. And there is no way in hell I could ever be just friends with you. Long distance or otherwise. You know why, Carmen?" He reached for her, grabbing her shirt and snatching her hard in a hot crush against his chest while she watched on with wide eyes. "Because I'm still in love with you, damn it! If I can't have it all, I don't want any of you. Because a mere taste of friendship or seeing you here and there would never be enough to fulfill the craving inside of me for you."

He continued to pull her tightly, almost violently to him, sealing her in his arms as his lips delved into to hers, stealing the very breath she inhaled with his invading tongue. Her feet backpedaled, almost tripping over herself as she stammered from his conquering undertaking. A squeal slipped from her throat, but it was muddled by the covering of his stinging kiss. A blazing fire torched through them, and simultaneously, their hands hurried to peel off the clothes that separated their flesh. The items went flying overhead, across the room and to the base of their feet as they wiggled and shimmied, desperate to connect with one another once again. Her skin tingled when he touched her with an occasional jolt lightning her up like molten lava. The weight of his massive dick pressed so roguishly against her belly that a trembling moan escaped her mouth.

His tongue traced down her chin where he sank his teeth in her flesh and growled like a starving animal that had cornered his prey and was preparing for a feast. Hot palms smacked her ass, and with a quick lift, Carmen's legs were wrapped around his waist just as his rock-hard cock impaled her womb. It spread through her pussy as if breaking the seal for the first time, causing her head to fall back and her mouth to open on a squeal.

"Oh my God, Dominic!"

He rocked into her core with hands stitched against her derriere and fervent thrusts that demanded her submission. He was like an unrelenting miner, tunneling through her womb with hardcore strokes that pinged off her G-spot, making her come with a rushing wave of spirited orgasms on impact.

"Oooooh my God!" she cried as her toes curled and her jaw locked.

Dominic dropped kisses down her throat and sucked in a nipple as his hips rocked back and forth, in and out, round and round, uncultivated like a savage with no precaution of the clemency her body currently screamed for. The attack was certifiably carnal, unfettered, and agile, taking Carmen through the depths of passion that remained uncensored, outlandish, and rogue.

"I love you, I love you, I love you," he chanted, licking up her chest only to sink his fangs into the flesh of her neck.

Carmen had never come so much. With her body on

a constant vibrating frequency, her mouth open, and in response she whined, "I love you, too, Dominic!"

He continued to thrash inside her, and she coated his dick with warm crème, making their ride a slippery slope. When he came, the sound that trekked from his throat was like a anguished cry, and his grip became a force that nearly tore through her flesh.

"Fuuuuuuuu-ck!" he screamed.

Carmen's entire body quaked as she rained kisses down his face, nose, and lips. At his mouth, she spoke. "I love—" He sucked her in, stealing her native tongue and running off with her speech. The devouring was profound, succulent, and dangerously delicious. The fulfillment was an overflowing waterfall for them both, tangling them in a release so beautiful they desired to stay that way forever. They were still trying to comprehend the magnitude of everything they'd just shared, but no matter the length of time, they remained joined in each other's arms. But time waited for no one, and it moved, forcing Dominic and Carmen to move with it.

FIVE A.M. CAME SO SWIFTLY IT WAS LIKE A BLINK OF THE eye, but yet, there they stood, in front of Brunswick Golden Isles Airport, staring at each other hand in hand.

"It seems like just yesterday that I got here," Carmen joked with a thin smile.

Dominic chuckled. "Yeah, twenty-four hours isn't a whole lot of time," he drawled.

Carmen reached for his chin and caressed his face with the palm of her hand.

"Thank you for being there for me." She hesitated. "I'm going to miss you."

Her voice was soft with a weary air of sadness tucked in the middle. Dominic inhaled a hard breath and reached for the hand that covered his face. His fingers slipped into hers, and slowly, he floated her hand to his mouth for a kiss. The warmth from his lips made Carmen shudder, but it wasn't the only thing that shook at the moment. Currently, her entire insides were jumbled, and her nerves ran a marathon of crazed activity through her.

This was it. She was leaving, and Dominic hadn't made an attempt to change his mind about them pursuing friendship once she was gone. It saddened her so bad her heart ached, and tears threatened to spill from her eyes.

Seeing her sadness, Dominic reached for her chin and lifted her face to him.

"Hey, everything's going to be okay. Your grandmother is in a better place. I'm sure she'll always be watching over you."

Carmen opened her mouth to speak, but she decided it may not sound the best if she confessed that her tears weren't for Grandma Mitchell at all. Instead, she nodded.

"Thanks again for being there for me," she said. "I'll always cherish that."

Dominic's mouth tightened along with his chest, and he nodded. He dropped his hand and, without another word, reached for her fingers to pull her along. They strolled unhurriedly into the airport where they were stopped at a security checkpoint.

Dominic cleared his throat. "Well, this is where we part," he said. His arms reached around her shoulders, and with a pull, his embrace cocooned her snugly. Carmen returned his hug, resting her chin in the crook of his neck as her eyes closed. Their heartbeats harmonized as they stood still feeling indifferent about their farewell. After Dominic released her, he slipped his hands inside his pockets and forced himself not to touch her again.

Carmen smiled.

"Have a safe flight," he said.

She nodded, then entered the checkpoint with Dominic watching. Once she made it to the other side, she turned and gave him two thumbs up. He nodded with a tilt of his head and a soft lingering smile on his lips. It was then that he turned and walked away, heading back out the doors to his Durango.

Inside the terminal, Carmen's oxygen had been clogged by the huge knot in her throat. On autopilot, she strolled to the gate and returned the stewardess' greeting as she entered and found her seating.

"Ma'am, would you like me to put your bag in the overhead bin?" another stewardess asked.

Carmen nodded wordlessly and took her gaze to the right to stare at the tarmac below. Was it unrealistic to feel as if she'd just witnessed two deaths? One of a physical matter and the other emotional? What kind of sense did it make to have the money, the career, the friendships, if in turn all of that mounted into missing out on the love of your life?

Why was she on this plane? Could she leave and never look back?

Carmen asked herself all of these questions just as the loudspeaker grabbed their attention and spoke of the weather, their destination, and the seconds they had left till takeoff. Her spirit wanted to stay, but her feet never moved. Instead, she sat, forcing herself not to become a spectacle and deal with the fact that this was it; she and Dominic were over.

Her breathing became labored, and her pulse quickened just as the loudspeaker came back on and the captain spoke, "Ladies and gentlemen, it seems we have a problem at the gate. This will only be a short delay. Thank you for your patience."

Carmen frowned, and other passengers whispered in response to the captain's announcement. When Carmen shifted in her seat, she turned like the others to try and get a look out at the gate, but her view was blocked by

Dominic gliding through the door of the aircraft. Her lungs expanded on an intake of deep breaths that punctuated her with fresh air that Carmen was unaware she needed. Her eyes bucked, and her mouth opened at the determination on his edgy face.

"Dominic!" she said. Her hands dropped to her side. "What are you doing here?"

He meandered through the aisle of the plane to stand right in front of her.

"I need you to get off this flight," he said.

Carmen's heart rocked. "What—what're you talking about?" she stammered.

"You can't leave. This thing between you and me, it isn't a bump in the road. It's inevitable, and I'd be a fool to let you disappear from my life again."

He dropped down to one knee, and Carmen's eyes widened, and her mouth fell open as his gaze pleaded into her soul. "I don't have a ring right now, but I can get you one. Let me," he paused and dropped his head then lifted it back to her. "Stay," he said. "Let me love you, forever."

A tremor rocked her soul, and tears fell from her eyes.

"Oh my God!"

Her hands flew to her mouth, and she leaned forward and fell into his wide chest where she was covered by his strong arms.

"Please, baby, please, don't leave me," he begged.

Her cries worried him for a second, but the nod of her head gave him relief.

"I never wanted to leave. I want to stay," she whined.

"So you'll give me a lifetime then? I need you. I always have."

She nodded vigorously. "Yes, Dominic!"

He stood to his feet, pulling her with him as the passengers around them cheered them on with congratulations.

A woman watching them from the middle seat turned to her fiancé. "That should've been you chasing after me, as much as I've put up with yo' ass," she huffed.

Her fiancé rolled his eyes. "Shush, woman, messing up somebody else's moment," he grumbled.

But Dominic and Carmen couldn't have cared one iota. They were entrapped in the bliss of one another. Excited to start anew together, eternally.

EPILOGUE

Three months later

"I DO."

A deafening round of applause ran through the friends and family as they all witnessed the matrimony of Dominic and Carmen on the lawn of St. Simon's Lighthouse. The sun sat bright, and a stretch of fresh cut grass housed white picket chairs, barrels of ice with cold water, and a gazebo that was lodged stationary with the bride and groom inside. With an elated smile on her face, Carmen rubbed her small protruding belly while reveling that their little bundle in the oven was able to experience their family joining as one. The French set diamond encrusted band sparkled on her ring finger with white stones so sharp the fourteen karats could blind the entire wedding party.

Their wedding could've happened much sooner, but Dominic felt it was necessary that they hash out their differences with Carmen's grandfather. He'd made it his business to confront the old man head-on, and after a big blow out where Dominic had managed not to kill him, Benjamin had agreed to attend counseling. He was in serious need of removing the blame in his heart on his granddaughter for his daughter's loss and misfortune. And after the first two months in therapy, Ben had come over and apologized genuinely for the things he done and said to Carmen growing up. It was something that she never thought would happen. But that day, she looked at her fiancé only to realize that she loved him more than she ever thought one could love another person.

It was an easy decision to continue her modeling career from Brunswick. She'd taken more flights out to New York than ever before but with Dominic at her side she enjoyed every minute of it.

Her heart was full, and when the pastor asked her that fundamental question, the only other answer in the world was, "I do."

Carmen glanced at Mrs. Johnson, and her new mother-in-law winked.

Mrs. Johnson leaned toward her husband. "I tried to tell her," she said to him, causing Mr. Johnson to grumble in laughter.

"I'm sure you did, honey."

More thunderous applause scattered about, and Dominic reached for Carmen's veil then lifted it, and when his lips crushed into hers, his hand slipped to her stomach with a caressing rub.

"I love you," he said against her mouth. He dropped his forehead into Carmen's and glanced down at her belly. "And you, too."

Carmen smiled so hard her cheeks burned.

"We love you, too, now and forevermore."

I HOPE YOU ENJOYED THIS FIRST BOOK IN THE LUNCH Break Series, If I Could Stay. Subscribe to my newsletter or join my Facebook Group to get updates from me, the author!

Reviews are the lifeblood of independent writers. The more reviews we get, the more Amazon and others promote the book. If you want to see more books by me, Stephanie Nicole Norris, a review would let me know that you're enjoying the series. If you liked the book, I ask you to write a review on Amazon!

Connect with Me on Facebook!
Connect with Me on Instagram!

OTHER BOOKS BY STEPHANIE NICOLE NORRIS

Contemporary Romance

- Everything I Always Wanted (A Friends to Lovers Romance)
- Safe with Me (Falling for a Rose Book One)
- Enough (Falling for a Rose Book Two)
- Only If You Dare (Falling for a Rose Book Three)
- Fever (Falling for a Rose Book Four)
- A Lifetime with You (Falling for a Rose Book Five)
- She said Yes (Falling for a Rose Holiday Edition Book Six)
- Mine (Falling for a Rose Book Seven)
- The Sweetest Surrender (Falling for a Rose Book Eight)
- Tempted By You (Falling for a Rose Book Nine)
- No Holds Barred (In the Heart of a Valentine Book One)
- A Risqué Engagement (In the Heart of a Valentine Book Two

Romantic Suspense Thrillers

- Beautiful Assassin
- Beautiful Assassin 2 Revelations
- Mistaken Identity
- Trouble in Paradise
- Vengeful Intentions (Trouble in Paradise 2)
- For Better and Worse (Trouble in Paradise 3)
- Until My Last Breath (Trouble in Paradise 4)

Crime Fiction

- Prowl
- Prowl 2
- Prowl 3
- Hidden

Fantasy

- Golden (Rapunzel's F'd Up Fairytale)

Non-Fiction

- Against All Odds (Surviving the Neonatal Intensive Care Unit) *Non-Fiction

ABOUT THE AUTHOR

Stephanie Nicole Norris is an author from Chattanooga, Tennessee, with a humble beginning. She was raised with six siblings by her mother Jessica Ward. Always being a lover of reading, during Stephanie's teenage years, her joy was running to the bookmobile to read stories by R. L. Stine.

After becoming a young adult, her love for romance sparked, leaving her captivated by heroes and heroines alike. With a big imagination and a creative heart, Stephanie penned her first novel *Trouble in Paradise* and self-published it in 2012. Her debut novel turned into a four-book series packed with romance, drama, and suspense. As a prolific writer, Stephanie's catalog continues to grow. Her books can be found on her website and Amazon. Stephanie is inspired by the likes of Donna Hill, Eric Jerome Dickey, Jackie Collins, and more. She currently resides in Tennessee with her husband and three-year-old son.

https://stephanienicolenorris.com/

CPSIA information can be obtained
at www.ICGtesting.com
Printed in the USA
LVHW082111121118
596842LV00015B/369/P

9 781720 265030